W9-AWP-283

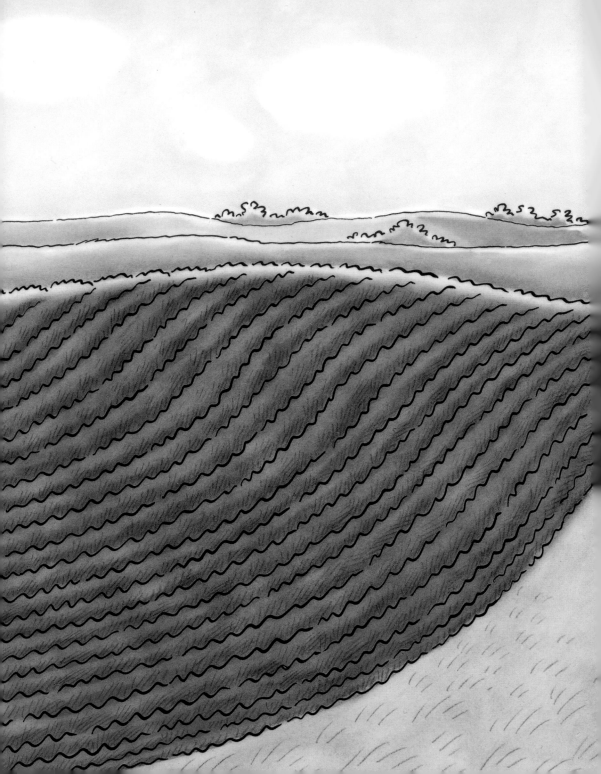

ALADDIN PAPERBACKS
An imprint of Simon & Schuster Children's Publishing Division
1230 Avenue of the Americas, New York, NY 10020
Copyright © 1995 by Lisa Campbell Ernst

ALADDIN PAPERBACKS and colophon are registered trademarks of
Simon & Schuster, Inc.
Also available in a Simon & Schuster Books for Young Readers
hardcover edition.
Designed by Lisa Campbell Ernst
The text of this book was set in Avant Garde.
The illustrations were rendered in pastel, ink, and pencil.
Manufactured in the United States of America
First Aladdin Paperbacks edition September 1998
Second Aladdin Paperbacks edition January 2005
2 4 6 8 10 9 7 5 3
The Library of Congress has cataloged the hardcover edition as follows:
Ernst, Lisa Campbell. Little Red Riding Hood: a newfangled prairie
tale/written and illustrated by Lisa Campbell Ernst.
p. cm.
Summary: An updated version, set on the prairie, of the familiar story
about a little girl, her grandmother, and a not-so-clever wolf.
ISBN 0-689-80145-9 (hc.)
(1. Fairy tales. 2. Folklore.) I. Title
PZ8.E7Li 1995 (398.21)—dc20 94-45723
ISBN 0-689-87831-1 (Aladdin pbk.)

Thanks to Jillian, Sally,
and The Ellis School!

For
Elizabeth

LITTLE RED RIDING HOOD
A Newfangled Prairie Tale

LISA CAMPBELL ERNST

ALADDIN PAPERBACKS
New York London Toronto Sydney

Once upon a time there was a little girl who lived at the edge of a great prairie. Because she always wore a jacket with a red hood when she rode her bike, everyone called her Little Red Riding Hood.

Now one morning, as Little Red Riding Hood sat eating her favorite wheat berry muffins, she had an idea.

"Mom," she said, "it's going to be a real scorcher today. Grandma sure would love it if I brought her some muffins and lemonade. You know how crabby she gets in the heat." Little Red Riding Hood loved visiting her grandmother.

"Great idea," her mother said.

So Little Red Riding Hood's mother packed the still-warm wheat berry muffins and cold lemonade into a basket.

After airing up the tires on her bike and testing the brakes, Little Red Riding Hood set out on her way.

"Now don't forget," called her mother. "Go straight to Grandma's, and whatever you do, don't talk to strangers."

"Sure, Mom," Little Red Riding Hood promised.

Little Red Riding Hood pedaled down Toad Road, past the gas station, the feed store, and the old Wilson place. She waved at everyone she saw, and everyone waved back.

As the edge of town disappeared, and the prairie began, Little Red Riding Hood zigzagged between the crops, taking the shortcut to Grandma's house. Blackbirds startled and sunflowers swayed as she whizzed by.

"What a nice visit this will be," Little Red Riding Hood said. "Grandma simply adores muffins and lemonade."

But who should be cutting through that same field — and up to no good, I might add — but a very hungry wolf.

When the smell of those wheat berry muffins came wafting his way, the wolf's nose quivered. "Gadzooks!" he whispered. "What is that scrumptious smell?"

The wolf rushed toward the heavenly odor. "Whatever it is, I must have it," he growled.

With one giant leap, the wolf landed right in front of Little Red Riding Hood's bicycle.

"Aha!" he roared.

Little Red Riding Hood slammed on her brakes. "Hey! Be careful!" she shouted. "You could get hurt surprising someone like that!"

The wolf chuckled at the warning. "What's in the basket, dearie?" he asked with a wide-toothed grin.

"Muffins and lemonade," Little Red Riding Hood said slowly, "for my grandmother."

"But such a tantalizing smell," the wolf drooled. "They must be *very special* muffins!"

"Oh, they are!" Little Red Riding Hood said proudly. "They're my grandma's secret recipe, and they always take first prize at the fair."

The wolf licked his lips. "She must be a dear, sweet woman," he crooned. "Do you have very far to travel?"

"Oh no," Little Red Riding Hood answered, "just over that ridge, this side of Turkey Creek."

"Mmm-hmm," the wolf smirked, his mouth curling up at the corners. "How fortunate."

"I have to go," Little Red Riding Hood said quickly. "Grandma's waiting."

The wolf slyly turned in the opposite direction and pointed. "Ooooh," he gasped. "What beautiful flowers! Such a dear, sweet grandmother *surely* deserves some of those!"

Little Red Riding Hood nodded. "Gee, you're right," she said, jumping off her bike, "Grandma loves flowers. Do you think she'd like these white ones, too?"

But the whistle of the prairie wind was the only response. The wolf was gone.

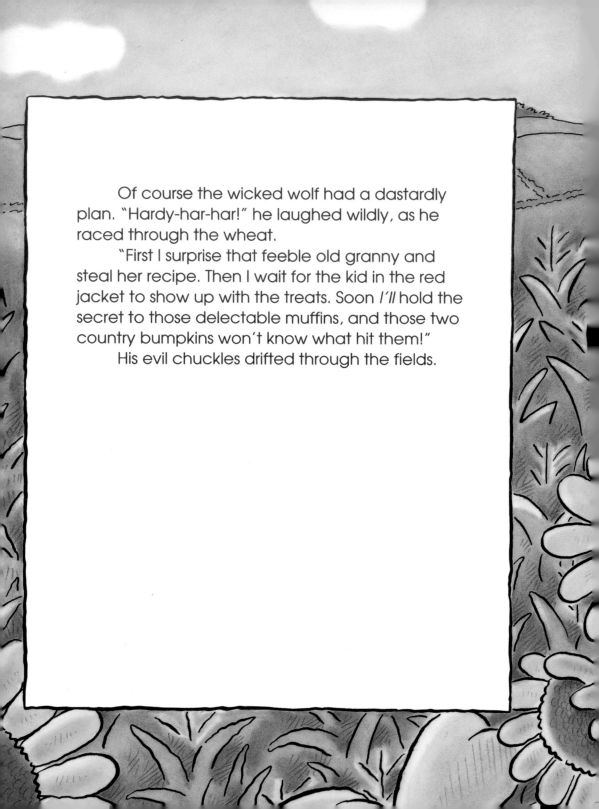

Of course the wicked wolf had a dastardly plan. "Hardy-har-har!" he laughed wildly, as he raced through the wheat.

"First I surprise that feeble old granny and steal her recipe. Then I wait for the kid in the red jacket to show up with the treats. Soon *I'll* hold the secret to those delectable muffins, and those two country bumpkins won't know what hit them!"

His evil chuckles drifted through the fields.

When the wolf arrived at Grandma's house, he found a note on the door.

Little Red Riding Hood –
Out in the field.
Love,
Grandma

"This will be easier than I thought!" the wolf snarled. "Grandma's obviously off her rocker, wandering around in the heat. Muddled brains are so easy to persuade!" The wolf cackled, feeling enormously pleased with his good fortune.

But when the wolf searched the fields for Little Red Riding Hood's tottering granny, all he could see was a farmer riding a tractor.

Impatient, he shouted. "Hey! Old man! Where's the ancient granny who lives in the house?"

The farmer, though, seemed to hear nothing. "Very well," the wolf said with a snicker. "I love surprising these dim-witted hicks." And he began to silently sneak up behind the tractor.

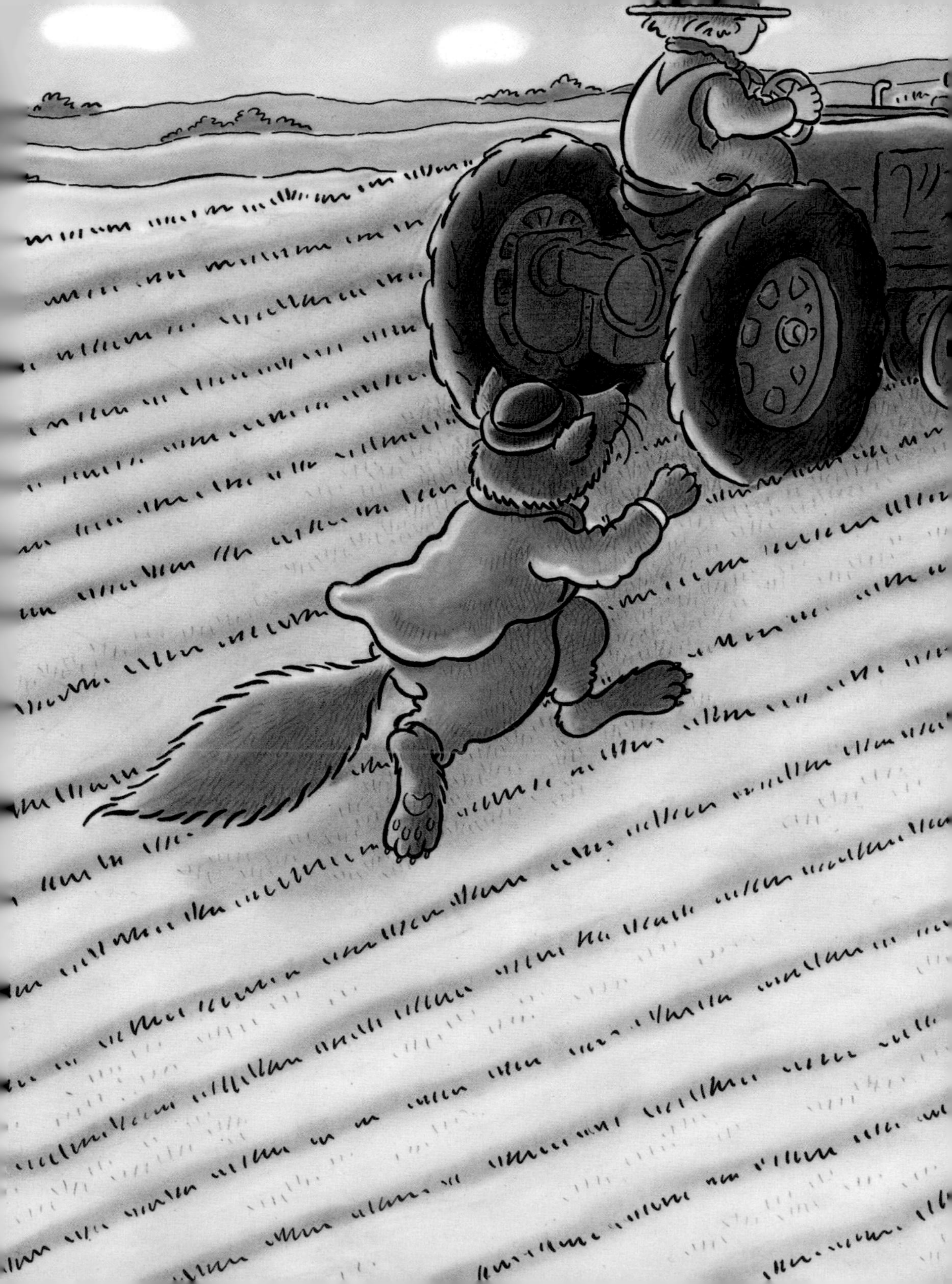

Then — before the wolf knew what was happening — the farmer whirled around and grabbed him by his fancy suspenders.

"Hold it right there, scoundrel!" the farmer shouted. "What in tarnation do you think you're doing?"

The wolf gasped and stammered, "I-I-I'm looking for the frail, loony, muffin-baking granny who lives in the house."

"Well, Sherlock!" boomed the farmer, whose grip tightened on the wolf. "*You're talking to her!*"

The wolf's mouth dropped open, and he began to shake. "M-m-my," he finally whispered, "what big *eyes* you have, Grandma."

"All the better to *see* you, skulking around my fields!" Grandma answered.

"My, what big *ears* you have, Grandma," the wolf croaked.

"All the better to *hear* you coming," Grandma answered.

"My, what big *hands* you have, Grandma," the wolf groaned.

"All the better to crush you like a bug, if need be," said Grandma. And, lucky for the wolf, Little Red Riding Hood rolled up just at that moment.

"Grandma, are you OK?" called Little Red Riding Hood.

"Sure, sweetie," Grandma said.

Together, they marched the grumbling wolf to Grandma's kitchen, Grandma lecturing all the way. "Didn't you think if there was a Little Red Riding Hood there might be a *Big* Red Riding Hood? I thought I got rid of bullies like you when I moved away from that forest!

"Might as well have a bite to eat while we decide what to do next," Grandma said. The wolf for once was silent, his mouth full of the delicious muffins.

"Of *course*," Grandma said at last.

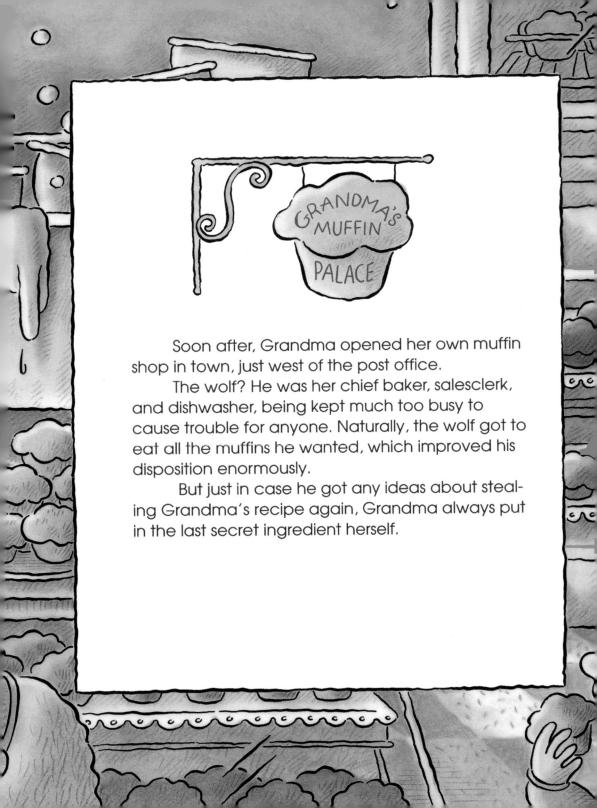

Soon after, Grandma opened her own muffin shop in town, just west of the post office.

The wolf? He was her chief baker, salesclerk, and dishwasher, being kept much too busy to cause trouble for anyone. Naturally, the wolf got to eat all the muffins he wanted, which improved his disposition enormously.

But just in case he got any ideas about stealing Grandma's recipe again, Grandma always put in the last secret ingredient herself.

Little Red Riding Hood, too, went to work for her grandmother, delivering muffins on her bike.

Every day, rain or shine, the wolf carefully packed Little Red Riding Hood's basket.

"Hey, kid!" he called after her as she whizzed down Toad Road. "Don't talk to strangers!"

And Little Red Riding Hood never did again.

Grandma's Wheat Berry Muffins
makes about 12 muffins

If your Grandma's not around to help you make
these tasty morsels, find someone who can!

2 eggs   ½ cup melted butter or margarine   1 cup sugar
½ tsp. almond extract   1 cup wheat flour   1 cup white flour
1 tsp. baking powder   ½ tsp. salt   2 cups blueberries
¼ cup sunflower seeds   (Grandma's secret ingredient)

First turn on the oven to 350 degrees. In a large bowl, mix together
the eggs, butter, sugar and almond extract. In another bowl, mix
the flour, baking powder and salt. Add that to the egg mixture
and stir just until combined. Gently stir in the blueberries and
the secret ingredient after making sure there are no wolves lurking
about. Fill oiled muffin tins ¾ full, and bake for about 20 to 25
minutes. These muffins taste best when shared.